This book
belongs to:

_____

Bowler Hat Guy

Lewis

Wilbur
Robinson

STARRING

Doris

Goob

Grandpa Bud

First published by Parragon in 2007
Parragon
Queen Street House
4 Queen Street
Bath BA1 1HE, UK

ISBN 978-1-4054-8447-3

Printed in Italy

DISNEY
MEET THE
ROBINSONS

Bath • New York • Singapore • Hong Kong • Cologne • Delhi • Melbourne

Lewis was an orphan. He desperately wanted a family, but no one would adopt him. In fact, he'd already had one hundred and twenty four rejections.

"That boy is not right for us," couples would say, and they would leave the orphanage without him. Some even ran!

The trouble was, Lewis was a bit different from the other kids. He loved inventing things, but when he demonstrated his latest prototypes – like the Peanut-Butter-and-Jelly Sandwich Maker – a lot of them didn't work. Well, to be honest, most of them blew up...big time.

Lewis's hopes of finding a family were fading. And this made him very sad. He'd often sit all alone on the roof of the orphanage, wondering why his mother had abandoned him when he was a baby.

One day, Lewis had the inspiration for an invention that would help him remember his past – a Memory Scanner! He hoped that it would help him find his mum. And if he found her, then maybe they could become a family.

Lewis's teacher, Mr Willerstein, encouraged the young inventor to enter his Memory Scanner in the school science fair. Night after night, Lewis stayed up planning and researching, welding, hammering and sawing, much to his room-mate's annoyance!

Mike "Goob" Yagoobian couldn't sleep at all. Not even the night before his big championship baseball game!

On the morning of the game, Lewis put the finishing touches to his invention…and a very tired Goob headed out to the baseball field, hoping he could stay awake.

When Lewis arrived at the science fair, the judges were already lined up: Mr Willerstein, Dr Krunklehorn (a scientist from Inventco Labs) and the school coach.

Lewis was starting to set up his Memory Scanner, when a boy he'd never seen before grabbed him and pulled him under the blanket that was covering his invention.

"Special Agent Wilbur Robinson of the Time Continuum Task Force," the stranger said. "I'm here to protect you."

He went on to explain that a tall man in a bowler hat had stolen a Time Machine and was now after Lewis! Lewis didn't believe him – in fact, he thought the stranger was crazy!

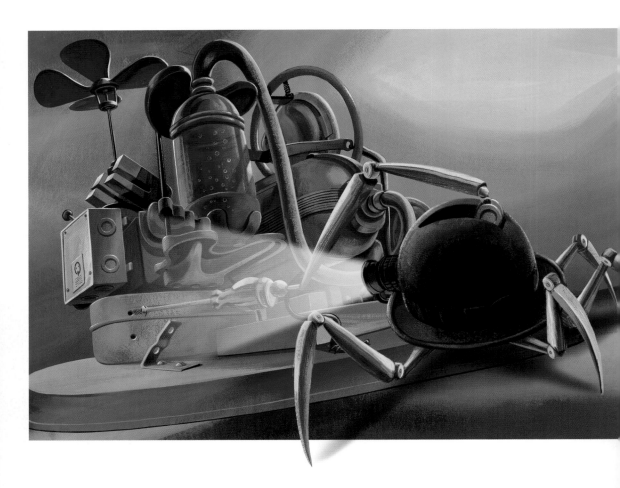

With the science fair in full flow, the Bowler Hat Guy set his plan in motion. The villain's hat – which was really a robot called Doris – flew over to Lewis's project. She slipped under the blanket covering the Memory Scanner and began to tinker with Lewis's invention.

As the judges moved closer, Doris worked frantically to sabotage the machine. Lewis was too nervous – and still too puzzled at what Wilbur had told him – to notice.

When the judges finally reached his table, Lewis proudly unveiled his Memory Scanner. He felt confident and very excited – soon, he'd remember his mum, then he could find her and they would become a family.

Lewis was just starting his demonstration when Wilbur caught sight of Doris scurrying across the floor. He knew something bad was about to happen,

"LEWIS! WAIT!" he shouted.
But it was too late…

Disaster struck! The fan flew off the Memory Scanner. It hit the lights and set off the gym sprinklers, causing chaos everywhere.

Lewis was devastated. Not only had his invention failed, but he had ruined the science fair and disappointed his teacher, too. Totally dejected, he ran out of the gym.

Wilbur found Lewis up on the roof tearing pages from his notebook and vowing never to invent again. He was desperate to get Lewis back to the science fair to fix the Memory Scanner. But Lewis refused.

So Wilbur pushed him over the side of the roof! Lewis screamed, then – THUNK – he landed on something solid and invisible! Wilbur joined him, pushed a button and revealed a Time Machine.

The boys struck a deal – if Wilbur proved he was really from the future, Lewis would return to the science fair and fix his invention.

Suddenly, Lewis found himself surrounded by monorails, flying cars and people travelling inside giant bubbles. He was in the future! And, according to Wilbur, it was all invented by Cornelius Robinson – Wilbur's dad!

Lewis was very excited. The Time Machine could take him back to the moment his mum left him on the orphanage steps.

But Wilbur was determined to return Lewis to the science fair to repair the Memory Scanner.

The boys began to fight for the controls and the Time Machine plunged to the ground. CRASH!

Dizzy, but unhurt, the boys stared at the wrecked machine. "You fix it," Wilbur said. They struck another deal – Lewis would repair the Time Machine and in return, Wilbur would take him to see his mum.

Meanwhile, back in the past, amid the chaos at the science fair, Doris had helped Bowler Hat Guy steal the malfunctioning Memory Scanner. He was now in the boardroom of Inventco Labs pretending it was his own invention.

But Bowler Hat Guy didn't know how to switch on the Memory Scanner. His presentation was a total flop and he soon realized that he needed Lewis's help to get his plan to succeed.

But where had the young inventor gone?

At the Robinson compound, Wilbur and Lewis pushed the broken Time Machine into the garage. Wilbur stuck a silly fruit hat on Lewis's head to hide his hairstyle so no one would know he was from the past, then told him to stay put.

Wilbur found Carl, the family robot, and quickly filled him in on their mission: they would convince Lewis to repair the Time Machine, which would restore his confidence in inventing, then they'd return him to the past to fix the Memory Scanner and restore the space-time continuum.

Carl told Wilbur that if he failed there was a 99.999999 percent chance that Wilbur would not exist.

"Wilbur Robinson never fails."

Wilbur confidently replied.

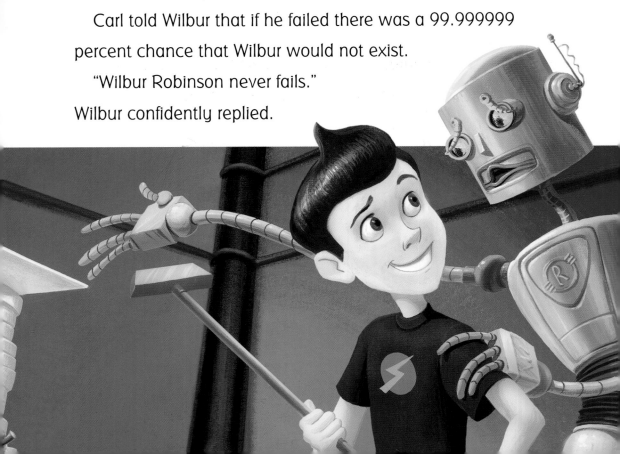

Meanwhile, in the garage, Lewis got sucked into a Travel Tube. He popped out on the front lawn beside Grandpa Bud, who was looking for his false teeth!

As Grandpa Bud lead Lewis back to the garage, they passed Uncle Gaston racing an enormous toy train by shooting himself out of a cannon. Then they watched Uncle Art blast off on an intergalactic pizza delivery. They saw cousin Laszlo zip overhead in his propeller helmet, splashing paint on cousin Tallulah's skyscraper hat. And they saw Uncle Fritz arguing with his hand-puppet wife, Petunia. But they didn't find Grandpa Bud's lost teeth – or the garage!

When they opened the last door, a blast of music greeted them. Wilbur's mum, Franny, was conducting a band of frogs!

Soon Lewis was joining in. He even spotted one of the frogs wearing Grandpa's false teeth!

The Robinsons were definitely different – but they were a lot of fun!

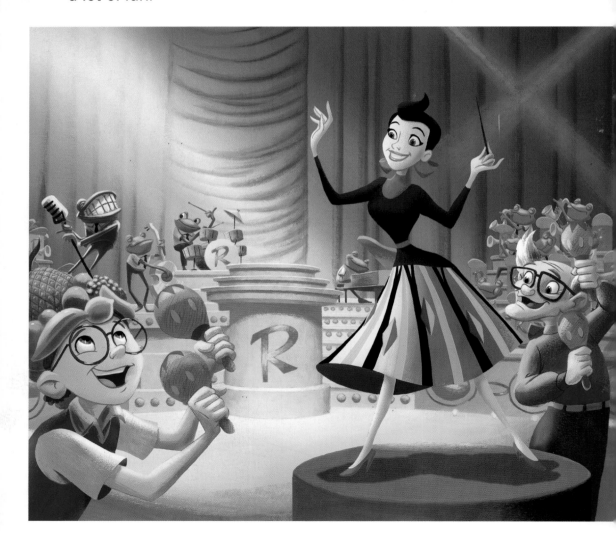

Eventually, Wilbur found Lewis and took him back to the garage and the broken Time Machine. "What if I can't fix this?" Lewis asked. Wilbur told him of Cornelius's motto: 'Keep Moving Forward'. Inspired, Lewis set to work on the machine. But when the boys tested it…it broke again.

At dinner with the Robinson family, Lewis couldn't help feeling like a failure. Suddenly, Carl appeared wearing a Peanut-Butter-and-Jelly Sandwich Maker! Unfortunately, it malfunctioned, so Wilbur asked Lewis to fix it. When he turned it back on, the machine exploded, but the Robinsons all cheered. Lewis was confused, but then he realized that failure wasn't bad. It just meant you should try again!

Outside, Bowler Hat Guy was watching. He and Doris had used the stolen Time Machine to come to the future and capture Lewis. On the villain's command, a dinosaur came crashing through the Robinsons' window. It was being mind-controlled by Bowler Hat Guy and tried to swallow Wilbur whole...but it wasn't long before Lewis rescued him.

The Robinsons were overjoyed. "You are a very special kid," they all declared.

And then it happened: Wilbur's mum asked Lewis if he wanted to be a Robinson!

Lewis couldn't believe his luck! But Wilbur panicked. He had no choice but to take off Lewis's hat and reveal that he was from the past.

The Robinsons gasped. "I'm sorry," Franny said. "You have to go back to your own time."

Lewis was distraught. Wilbur still hadn't fulfilled his promise to take him to see his mum.

Angrily, Franny turned to Wilbur, "You promised what?!"

"I was never gonna do it!" Wilbur said, looking guilty.

Poor Lewis. It was the worst rejection yet, and on top of everything, Wilbur had lied to him. He ran off in tears.

Suddenly, Bowler Hat Guy appeared and offered Lewis a deal. He and Doris would take Lewis to find his mum if Lewis agreed to fix the Memory Scanner. Silently, Lewis climbed into the Time Machine and was transported to Bowler Hat Guy's lair – Lewis and Goob's old room at the orphanage.

Lewis fixed the Memory Scanner, but instead of taking him to meet his mother, Bowler Hat Guy ordered Doris to tie the boy up!

Then Bowler Hat Guy ripped off his cape to reveal a child's tattered baseball uniform. "It is I, Mike Yagoobian!" he announced.

"Goob?!" cried Lewis. "How'd you end up like this?"

Bowler Hat Guy told Lewis that he'd never got over falling asleep during the baseball game and losing the championship.

He stayed at the orphanage his whole life, feeling more and more bitter and jealous as Lewis became successful.

Then Goob met Doris. Together, they stole the Time Machine and travelled to the past to steal the Memory Scanner and ruin Lewis's future.

Finally, Lewis understood! In the future, he would become Cornelius Robinson – Wilbur's dad! And Doris's bitterness towards him was because she was one of Cornelius Robinson's rejected inventions.

"Now, all that's left is to return to Inventco, where I'll pass off your little gizmo as my own!" laughed Bowler Hat Guy as he dragged Lewis and the Scanner to the roof.

Suddenly, Lewis heard Wilbur's signal, "Coo, coo!" Wilbur and Carl were high in the air thanks to Carl's stretchy robot legs. Lewis pushed the Memory Scanner off the roof and jumped, landing safely in Carl's outstretched arms.

Doris and Bowler Hat Guy followed the trio towards the Robinsons' home. Suddenly, Doris attacked Carl and snatched the Memory Scanner. Then the two villains blasted back towards the past.

Wilbur and Lewis were horrified. The entire future was at risk, and they were stuck with nothing but a broken Time Machine.

Wilbur pleaded with Lewis to fix the Time Machine, but Lewis didn't think he could. As they argued, Wilbur's voice faded. A swirling black cloud appeared in the sky and Wilbur disappeared into it!

Things were changing because in the past, Bowler Hat Guy was signing a contract with Inventco. Each stroke of his pen was changing the future. Lewis shouted for the Robinsons, but no one answered. Instead, he saw Doris's memories on what looked like an evil version of Lewis's Memory Scanner...and it showed the horrible future she had created.

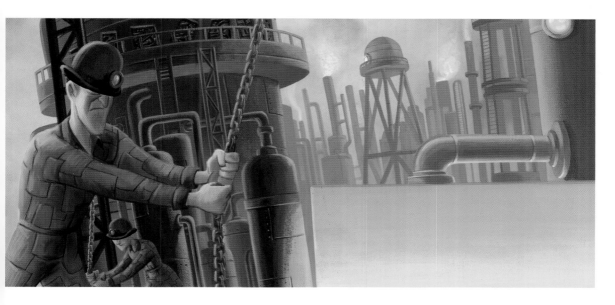

Frantically, Lewis began working on the Time Machine. At last, it roared into life and Lewis shot from the future and into the present day! He burst into the boardroom where Bowler Hat Guy was signing his name.

"Goob! Stop!" Lewis shouted and quickly explained Doris's evil plans. Goob only wanted to ruin Lewis, not the entire world!

Just then, Doris released her steely claws and came at Lewis. Then, with a firm look, Lewis said, "I am never going to invent you." With that, Doris disappeared forever and Bowler Hat Guy was just plain old Goob.

He and Lewis returned to the future and watched Doris's evil world turn bright and happy again. Then Goob walked away…it was time for him to find his own destiny.

signature…X

Just then, Cornelius Robinson appeared. Realizing who Lewis was, he gave the boy a tour of his lab and showed him the invention he was most proud of – the Memory Scanner! Lewis was amazed.

Then, Wilbur did something totally unexpected. He took Lewis to see his mum! Lewis watched as she placed a box on the orphanage doorstep. But meeting her might change the wonderful life and family he now knew awaited him in the future, so he jumped in the Time Machine and returned to the present.

After saying goodbye to Wilbur, Lewis raced to the baseball field and saw Goob asleep. "Goob! Wake up!" he shouted.

Goob awoke – and made the game-winning catch! He was a champ now and his future looked bright!

Back at the science fair, Lewis demonstrated the repaired Memory Scanner for the judges...and it worked! Dr. Krunklehorn put on the headset, set a date and saw wonderful memories of her wedding day.

When her husband, Bud Robinson, arrived to collect her, he winked at Lewis. "You don't look like a Lewis," he said. "You look more like a..."

"Cornelius!" interrupted Lewis.

Dr. Krunklehorn and Bud adopted Lewis. He knew they would be Grandma and Grandpa Robinson one day. They bought a house with a wonderful room for Lewis to work in – it would become his lab in the future.

At last, Lewis had a family.

And whatever happened, his future would be bright... just as long as he kept moving forward!